Hoa Pham, a psychologist by day, is the author of six books. *Vixen* was awarded the Best Young Writer award by the *Sydney Morning Herald*, and *The Other Shore* won the Viva La Novella Prize. Her play *Silence* was on the VCE Drama list in 2010.

She is also the founder of *Peril Magazine,* an Asian-Australian online arts and culture magazine (www.peril.com.au). She has received funding from the Australia Council of the Arts, been on an Asialink residency in Vietnam, fellowships at the Tyrone Guthrie Centre and the Goethe Institute Berlin. She has a doctorate in creative arts and holds masters degrees in creative writing and psychology.

OTHER BOOKS BY HOA PHAM

No-one Like Me (1998)
49 Ghosts (1998)
Quicksilver (1999)
Vixen (2000)
Silence (2010)
The Other Shore (2014)

WAVE

HOA PHAM

SPINIFEX

For Alister, William and Max with love

Âu Cô

Inside it was warm like greenhouse flowers. Outside it was the end of the world.

At the start of the Buddhist 49 days of mourning, I remember you. Your little brother plays vigil at the shrine in your flat. Your picture smiles at me, your characteristic fish-hook smile caught me and the rest of the world. I remember what happened during the time I loved you. And despair.

Brother

He was waiting. Waiting for his mother to come. In his favourite yellow hat with the cosy ear flaps on and wrapped up in his red puffy parka.

They had just had open play time when they could do anything they liked. He made a picture for his mother out of autumn leaves. The brown foliage crunched in his hands and littered the paper with broken remains.

Usually Mummy would be on time. She would arrive and take his hand in hers and give him a kiss on the cheek. She smelt of perfume and newly applied lipstick. Then they would go home and have a hot chocolate while she cooked dinner.

He hoped she would come soon so he could give her his picture of leaves. He had made her a giraffe and a horse.

Outside was the distant roar of the ocean. Today he could hear the waves. It sounded like the beach had crept right up to their doorstep.

Next to him the other children were waiting too. No one's parents had arrived yet.

He was looking at the clock.

Soon they were all looking at the clock waiting for their parents to come.

The red digital numbers on the stark black clock told no lies.

Their parents were late.

He found himself thinking of his sister. Before she left for Australia she had been crying a lot in her room. She did not cry when their parents were home, she had been stiff faced. But when neither of them was there and she was supposed to look after him, she would retreat into her room and cry. He would sit in front of her sliding bedroom door and wait for her to come out for a cuddle.

His sister was beautiful, with cherubic short hair. She used to go to her friend's apartment a lot, but that stopped when the crying began. He missed his sister smiling and talking to him.

He looked back at the closed door to the children's room. No one's parents had arrived. That was strange. Sometimes one parent would be late. But all of them?

The children began whispering amongst themselves.

One child began to cry, snuffling softly.

Mother! He thinks into the ether, hoping that she can hear him shouting in his mind. Sometimes she does know, the hiccup before he cries out aloud that brings her running into his room. Other times she is deaf to him even when he is in her arms, warm and snug.

Where are all the mummies? Where have they gone?

A childcare worker opens the sliding door and is greeted by the silent anticipation of the children sitting in rows cross-legged on the floor.

She shakes her head, and now he can see how white she is and the deepest frown on her face close up. Something is wrong.

Âu Cô

I remember you the way you were, not the way you are.

We used to be we until they made us me and you.

I remember the first time I saw you. Your every movement was petite and curved, making me feel more clumsy and inept than before. But when you met my eye coming late into class, I was hooked by your smile.

We were partners in a group assignment. I usually hated group assignments, I could never work with my teammates and the Australian students never seemed to care. But with you, you were meticulous. Even after you confided in me that you found the English as a Second Language class not as difficult as English classes in Tokyo, you still were conscientious.

When you invited me over to your flat I was honoured. I took flowers, I had heard that Japanese were chronic gift givers. I also took chè, a desert of lychees and ginger. You oohed over the flowers and your little brother hogged the dessert. But I didn't care. You were nineteen and sophisticated. We had tonkatsu ramen for dinner and I felt privileged being let into your domestic world.

We chatted for hours. Even though I was from Hanoi and you were from Fukushima, we knew the same American rock bands, loved Miffy the cute rabbit and found Melbourne empty and alienating. You told me stories, smiling about misunderstandings with Australians. It made me laugh at my own insecurities, and I could share with you the silences that some Southern Việt Kiều greeted me with on hearing my Hanoian accent.

We had loneliness in common.

I spoke English with an American accent and that marked me forever as foreign.

I could not imagine the freedom of not living with adults. My aunt only let me stay over at your place because we had a class assignment. You were obligated, like I was, to do well at school because of our parents' money.

That night I was sleeping on the floor of your room when I heard you crying.

"What's wrong?" I asked.

"I hate it here," you said and automatically I withdrew. Maybe you hated being with me too.

"I'm so lonely. Please hug me."

I put my arms around you, so slight like a sparrow, and you nestled into me like a baby with her mother. Then you kissed me on the cheek and then the mouth, and I melted into you.

I want to be elsewhere. And to take you with me, you would say. An invitation for us to spin our own fantasies of what we could do once we earned enough of our own money.

I had never been to Japan. What you told me reminded me of a square puzzle box, of keeping up appearances, fencing in secrets, fencing in wants and desires.

You introduced me to anime, and cosplay. We began to write our own series of two girls against the rest of the world. We would be dragons, you and I. With sinewy serpentine bodies we were trapped in human form on earth for the transgression of loving each other and rebelling against our parents' wishes. Then you would make me fly with your fingers, and my back would arc in ecstasy.

We schemed together. We would wag classes that seemed unimportant, taught by fill-in-teachers who did not care. You were popular and would receive notes from the Japanese boys in the class. We would read them together and laugh. We would text when we were apart, using our dragon names, our secret names for each other.

I planned to go to Japan over summer to visit you. I did not want you to see my parents who did not know that you existed; nor my friends in Hanoi. Being in Australia was my freedom and I could not imagine any part of my Melbourne life being in Vietnam.

Midori

They breathe heavily, and fly at each other's touch. Her lover's fingers caress the petals of her inner self. She brushes her hands over her nipples for the fleeting sharp sensation. Then it is her lover's turn, and they sigh together, moisture mingling. From their union, a pearl is birthed from her throat. Her lover plucks the sweet gem from her mouth with her fingers. Slippery and wet the multi-coloured rainbow goes into her mouth and she swallows. They know that if anyone finds out about the gems they birth, they would no longer have the pleasure to themselves.

This is her memory, a reconstruction as she surges forward on her fingers remembering how to feel. She is gone now over the seas, exiled far away from all that is familiar.

I still love you. Even though they have separated us. I will never forget you.

Everything is a construction.

She wishes she were other than what she is. Tenses turn and twist as she remembers, sometimes she remembers the here and now, other times the past as she recalls it, in the quicksilver light of her teenage years.

When she orgasms she remembers the most. Memories flick by like comic book frames: the neon lights of Shinjuku out of a love hotel window, the fleeting kiss of loves that never were.

She would not exchange what she is for something else, she tells herself as she sinks into the hot bath scented with pink ginger. Her skin dissolves when she is in water and the warmth permeates her core.

When she was younger she and her first love would don costumes on Sundays and join the cosplay parading. She was slim and flat-chested and would go as Dragon Girl, a warrior in pigtails who had dragons slithering down her arms. She yearned to fly like Dragon Girl and her lover would go as Dragon Boy. That way business men would not try to proposition them as they did when her lover stayed true to her sex.

Others cannot forgive that she still holds memories of her first love dearest to her heart.

In Zen Buddhism the circle is emptiness and completeness. In Japanese literature, a mood is captured, a fleeting feeling. Unlike Western literature, it is not so important for the hero to conquer all.

She only began to play piano for her own pleasure once she was in Australia. There was an old upright piano in the corner of the multi-purpose meeting room in the apartment complex. No one could hear her, she did not have to think about what other people thought and felt. The sound bounced on the wooden floor, and the touch was uneven. Clunky though her renditions were, she lost herself in the tangled notes of her memory.

She has a younger brother. He is the only reason that she would not wish death on her parents. She had prayed to the old gods, the dragons of earth, water, fire and heaven.

When the dream came true she was terrified by the freedom she felt, falling into empty space.

Brother

He vanishes inside his mind.

A photographer taking their pictures, a flash of light over the children sitting in rows like temple statues. Then a red-headed white woman speaking a foreign language gives them soft toys.

He balances the brown soft toy kangaroo on his crossed legs. Outside older children are playing.

He remembers thinking, *They have not suffered. They do not know anything.*

Seriousness was pressed into him that day.

I'm not like them. I cannot be carefree.

He had the ever-present filial obligation to look after his older beautiful sister. Even though she had abandoned their ancestors and the family shrine.

Now the soft toy kangaroo is worn where his hand has clutched it every night in the foster home. One eye is missing but somehow the kangaroo yields to being squeezed in between his shirts and shoes in his suitcase.

What do you call the hopping mouse with a bag?

Kan-ga-rou.

Midori

Melbourne is the first place she can see the stars in the sky. She is stunned and spends nights lying on her back on the roof of the apartment complex gazing at the Southern Cross and the rabbit in the moon.

During the daytime the sky is electric blue, arcing overhead. The streets are empty. Without the mass of people to hold her in, she feels the boundaries of herself dissipate and fade.

At nineteen, she is the legal guardian of her brother. Australians think she is younger than she is; other Asians see the creases at the corner of her eyes and backs of her hands and say she is older. Since her parents died, guilt and responsibility make her shoulders tense and her hands ache with pain.

Her aunt accompanies her brother to Australia to see him settled in. She produces two framed photos of her parents for the family shrine, and buys incense for them to burn in her apartment.

Midori feels the censure from the stare of the photos. Even when deceased she cannot get away from her parents.

Her brother has retreated inside himself. She is cocooned in her own silence and shame. They live in the same apartment and eat the same brand of instant ramen together but each is alone.

New Years Eve. At home they would go to the shrine for luck and write their wishes on wooden tablets to hang up and blow in the breeze. Last New Years Day she was with her duet partner. They had bought identical pink outfits at the sales and pretended to be sisters, walking together with linked arms.

At the Inari temple they had posed for snapshots under a giant stone fox statue adorned with the red bib and wrote their dearest wishes for their love in kanji on fox-shaped tablets. Ringing the bells for luck they swore never to be parted and never to forget.

Music was her joy from when she was a toddler. She was taken to a Suzuki method concert when she was three. Little girls in white dresses played "Twinkle Twinkle Little Star" on the violin in unison, the youngest just two years old. Her mother asked her which instrument she would like to play and she said piano. There was only one pianist amongst the little girls, and she had always felt she was different from the rest.

Mother learnt alongside her at first, a memory that made her fingers ache in sympathy. Balancing 500-yen coins on the back of her hands to train her hands flat and straight. Doing five variations of "Twinkle Twinkle Little Star" and listening to the Suzuki repertoire on her MP3 player at night.

Then the recitals began, first in the guise of music camps. Guests to their home were treated to a little night music by Mozart. By then her mother had stopped shadowing her. She was eight when the competition began in earnest. She began to make up her own music, her own variations. Then one evening her mother, cooking in the next room, put down her chopping knife and walked into the room. The music jarred to a stop.

"What are you playing?"

"I'm making up a surprise for the teacher."

"Don't ever do that again. If you play that to the teacher how bad will I look? Concentrate on your recital."

Her mother left her, and so did the desire.

Her duet partner was assigned to her. A solemn girl, taller and four months older. Their mothers met, assessing each other under the teacher's supervision. The two girls practised together. The boundaries between them dissolved in the melding of their tunes. They won their first eisteddfod.

She rediscovered joy staying at her duet partner's house overnight. In this house they were allowed to read books past midnight. They exchanged clothing, and secrets. Her duet partner was taller, more awkward. But her breasts were budding like soft dumplings under her touch.

They played live to a TV studio audience to showcase their teacher. It was broadcast nationally and she was showered with attention for a day.

Their families went on excursions to the country together. They would share onsen in the hot springs, and share each other's stories. Then on one trip the mothers had an argument. Her mother, blushed with anger, told her they were going home early.

She never saw her duet partner again. She has been looking for her double, her collaborator, her muse ever since.

Brother

In his sister's shadow he blooms from benign neglect.

His sister taps on the computer keyboard late into the night, early into the morning. She is flat faced to her little brother but her phone beeps melodic messages constantly.

Their parents' legacy had already been earmarked for their education. Without being told, the siblings do what their parents would have wanted.

He watches his sister's movements. Sometimes she stays at university overnight and doesn't come home. He fails to say anything. Some nights he watches TV until she returns.

He becomes immersed in anime that he is familiar with in Japanese, which is dubbed into English. He is swallowed up by the characters and is taken by one androgynous lone hero, who sometimes is referred to as a girl, other times a boy. He styles his hair in the same shaggy cut and peroxides it blond.

No one is around to say no. She starts drinking lychee liquor in cans, imported from Japan. Then moves on to vodka and cordial. Sometimes she leaves empties around for him to finish off when she isn't looking.

Midori

Maybe this is why she cannot perform any more. The last time she drank a can of coffee before she was scheduled to play. She shook and sweated all over the keys. Then she disassociated, the audience dipped out of sight and she was far away, unable to access the joy that was once hers.

Her teacher was unsympathetic. The girl was a hard worker but fell apart under pressure. Soon the lessons ceased all together.

She does not realise that her mother's lies parallel hers.

He does not realise his destiny is preordained like tram tracks from the stories he emotes.

The stories between the lines and spaces on the pages.

She escaped to Australia, to get away from her parents whose scrutiny she failed to live up to. But once in the foreign land she found herself walled in by indifference. Only other international students wished to talk to her, especially the Japanese ones. The Australians, impatient with her barely adequate English, didn't care.

Midori had found a partner again, and the hard knot in her heart dissolved. There were differences, her lover's accent had rounded the corners of consonants, and their speech was moderated by their respective grasps of English. Sometimes it was an effort to speak, and she would murmur in Japanese before translating. She taught her ai

–愛–to say love. Chi yêu em were the first three Vietnamese words she learnt. I love you.

She wished death on her lover's parents too. No adults could understand what they had together and why they could not be apart.

In their secret universe they were water dragons, with the sea lapping against their scales. She was gold, her lover was silver and they were born of royalty. When they made love they produced precious pearls in their mouths, which humans and other creatures coveted. The dragon's pearl when ground up made for an immortal elixir. The dragons kept this secret or they would be hunted down for their pearls.

They went to St Kilda promenade, eating ice cream on the pier with the breeze blowing back their hair. Being Asian they could hold hands as best friends and curl up in the nook of each other's arms. The bay here was calm, glassy grey to blue. They looked at yachts and clambered on the black rocks of the escarpment. The sea air made Midori's skin edgy, and teased her lips and breasts.

"Look," she would exclaim and point to the sky.

The clouds spread out in a fan into the distance.

"Wind dragon," Âu Cô would say and the laughter would be shared and good.

Her little brother would watch them with solemn eyes. Legally his guardian she paid as much attention to him as necessary. He spent most of his time at home at the computer so she could ignore him.

Time flexes in her recollections, and her memories skew in other people's favour.

When they could not meet, they would tell stories. Chapters of stories, typed out on iPhones and computers, read on iPads and Kindles. The words were soft and the prose could not be caught in cyberspace. The adventures they would share if they could, of body and mind.

> Once there was a dragon that lived in the sea, her body formed sinewy by the beating of waves. She fell in love with the breeze above the water line that arced and kissed the ocean and the ground. Little did she know that it was a wind dragon that had caught her fancy because she was invisible in the sunlight. Only when she rippled across the water did her form become apparent by the shape of the waves.
>
> *Come to me*, the wind dragon would tease and the sea dragon would try to keep up with the moving air.
>
> Then the currents would change from warm to cold, and the waves would rise higher and higher. They would meet each other at the crest of waves and fly high in the arc before crashing down. But the

water dragon wanted to be with the wind dragon forever. She loved the entwining they would feel and longed for her when she was not there.

One day the sea drew back from the land, and the water dragon felt herself being dragged higher and higher.

Catch me! she said to the wind dragon, who had willed the air currents to match the pull of the ocean.

Then the tsunami came crashing down on the land. The water dragon who had risen higher than she had ever risen before, found herself hurtling down and her body crashed on buildings and cars and human beings. She shattered and broke roads apart. Buildings were sucked into the vortex of the ocean. When the ocean withdrew from the land she found herself being drawn back in, but this time she had caught the wind dragon with her coils in the water.

The wind dragon flew into the air accompanying the water dragon as she crashed onto the land again. They laughed together as they mingled as one, and revisited the shore again and again.

The wind dragon lost herself in the water dragon's coils but she did not mind because they were in love.

Midori watched as the story continued with her in its grasp. She did not know what to make of the tsunami appearing in their perfect, shared world. But it was true that the death of her parents had made their relationship more possible. She typed the words on her iPhone and tried not to think.

Âu Cô

The real world was far from perfect. I began to notice things about Midori. Little nicks and cuts on her arms and legs, razor sharp. I did not ask about them, because I did not want to know. All these things that in retrospect I should have said, and had been silent.

It was our shared escapes that made us special. Both of us could spin tales of dragons more fantastic than the last. Every breath of wind was a dragon chasing its tail. In the sky the spread of clouds was the wake of a dragon's flight. The dragons travelled the world in the realms of their imaginations.

Since I was young I had told stories, and arrogantly styled myself Âu Cô, the Mountain Fairy separated from Lạc Long Quân, the Dragon King. For the Vietnamese people that hatched from golden eggs, she would not reunite with her true love until the time of greatest need. My mother had instilled in me that I was to grow up, get married, have children and look after my parents when they grew old.

I fancied myself a mountain fairy grounded to earth for the greatest need.

Midori

The wave changed everything. She remembered where she was when the news came in. She was happy, listening to the radio. Her lover was slurping a smoothie of mango and she remembered the charge of seeing her and not touching her. Every glance was significant, and her breasts felt full and she felt attractive enough to flirt and tease.

Then the breaking news of the earthquake at Fukushima. And the tsunami.

She had gone on to the computer straight away for the Japanese newscasts. She had tried to call her parents but there was no coverage. She tried calling her little brother. Nothing.

The Japanese embassy was engaged for four hours before they had a voice mail message.

She was in shock. Her lover tried to comfort her, but now each touch was laden with guilt.

I wanted them to die. Now they are missing.

It was night before one of her aunts confirmed what she suspected all along. Her parents had died, and her brother luckily survived. Stay in Melbourne, her aunt said. It is chaos here.

She has to retell these stories so the therapist could fill in the blanks.

She was embarrassed to wake up.

If she looked back, she could tell the future. But in the present she could not see the water for the waves.

Narration is a form of hindsight. Everyone wants to make a story of their lives so it will all make sense. She knows this as she is typing on her iPad, the next chapter of their story without her.

The hospital is dull and neutral, like the nurses and doctors. There are other Asians who are Australians in her ward. No one makes eye contact; no one wants to be the first to do so. Having a morning walk around the park, forces her to communicate when all she wants to do is curl up inside and grieve. Not for her parents, but for her childhood and how safe she had felt.

She has to get out soon for her little brother. He would be so scared, and barely able to cook his own instant noodles. He had written her emails and texts saying he wants to visit and asking her why she wanted to leave him behind.

She still doesn't know the answer.

"I do want to live," she admits off-hand to the therapist, who nods.

What was the point of her liberation from her parents if she died as well?

What was the point of dreaming about dragons if one of them had lost her pearl?

What was the point?

Âu Cô

I was the first visitor to the ward that afternoon, carrying the largest bunch of white lilies I could afford, and a bag of Japanese sour candy.

“What do you think you were doing?” I exploded at Midori and threw the flowers at her.

“I was sad. Very sad.” Midori’s mouth doesn’t move, the words seem to crawl out between her lips.

Then the reality cascades on her and she cries. Our tears mingle together.

“Next time tell me how you are feeling.”

The unspoken vow: *Next time take me with you.*

“I was scared when your brother found you on the bathroom floor. How could you do this and not tell me how you were feeling?”

I was aware then of a force that was larger than you, that might take you away.

Truly, now you were free but you were like a kite on a string, tugging, tugging away. Then someone let go of your string and you spiralled out of control and were blown away.

Midori

She found the hospital was a good place not to think too much. It took her a while to understand what answers would see her released from hospital.

The support groups made her feel transparent like glass, which she only attended because her psychiatrist told her it was expected of her. The people in the groups were breakable like her.

She saw the psychiatrist as another well meaning Australian trying to teach her something. She let slip why her parents had sent her away and he jumped on their motivations as the reasons for all that had happened to her.

She did not understand. It was her fault that she was in exile. It took several sessions before she found the words to say that she was ashamed of her feelings of love. It seemed to make the psychiatrist happy.

Âu Cô

When you were in hospital I would pleasure myself in the depth of night after my aunt had gone to bed. To my surprise my body responded to the brushing of my fingers and then I would see you and your quirky smile. Then your sigh of contentment as I came.

In real life you were getting skinnier in the hospital. I brought you sushi and noodles which you ate in ravenous bites. I suddenly had time on my hands in the daytime before visiting hours. I visited your brother, on your request. He had made himself rice in the rice cooker and was eating it with tins of tuna. I took him in to see you. When you opened your arms to give him a hug he began to cry. I could understand the tone of what he was pleading with you in Japanese.

Don't leave me.

Brother

He thought that he was cursed. First his parents and then Midori tried to leave him all alone. The hospital social worker, who had a kind face and blond hair, asked him how he felt. No one had asked him that before and he found himself in tears again, like a melted snowman. He felt hollow like when the childcare worker told them that no one was going to pick them up, and he was never going to see his parents again.

She gave him a hug, the way Midori used to back in Japan and he cried until her blouse was wet.

Midori's Vietnamese friend was like her duet partner, at their apartment almost all the time. Her friends were more important to her than family, he was learning.

When he paid respect to his parents' photographs on the family shrine he thought of a photograph of Midori standing there and burst into tears again.

> Once upon a time there was a city. The city's inhabitants had performed acts of great evil, and murdered many people in gas ovens. When the enemies of the city had taken it over, the city was divided into four so the people would never murder again.
>
> A Wall was built like the spine of a dragon, dividing the city and the country into East and West. Many people came there from over the seas. Another country divided into North and South sent their brightest minds to the city. The people of the North were aligned with the East, and the South with the West.

One day a great ripple went along the Wall and the Wall was destroyed. East and West were united. But the people from the North and the people from the South still refused to acknowledge each other's existence. Some Walls cannot be traversed, even by dragons.

Sadness envelops her like a black hole. Nothing seems to come of being in the realms of depression. Thoughts – kamikaze suicidal thoughts – hem her in each day. The rare moments when she surfaces are grasping for air. The colour of autumn leaves, yellow and brown, stand out in her mood.

She just wants to sleep the pain away. Be free of thinking. She breathes in and swallows back tears. Even when on the beach with her lover and swimming in the sea she imagines drowning in a gentle sweeping away.

Her brother would be a hentai if he didn't have to come out of his bedroom to eat. She refuses to cook for him and leave the tray outside his door like some spoiling parents do. He comes out at night and from her room she can hear the ding of the microwave. Sometimes he leaves little notes for her. To her it proves that he is still trying to connect. Their aunt is the executor of their parents' estate which has been destroyed by the tsunami. She is constantly in contact with Midori's brother. Midori has brushed off her queries and concerns seeing just a younger version of her pushy mother.

Âu Cô

I always thought I was ugly. I was too tall and my face too broad to be called beautiful. Only around you did I appreciate the length of my legs, the darkness of my straight hair and the slight curves of my figure.

You were conventionally beautiful with an endearing hook of a smile. To you the world was full of wonder still. Your parents were the enemy, our peers were the gods and goddesses of our universe.

I saw the world through cracked glasses. I knew the government was corrupt, and that my loyalty to family and my parents was the only thing I could count on. The rest of the world was not my friend.

Like most beautiful people you thought that the rest of the world would always be nice to you, and you were surprised when things did not work out for you. You were popular and I could not see what you saw in me.

But one day while we were walking to your apartment from the university you confided in me.

I was the only one who knew you were lonely. I was the only one who kept your secrets. I was quiet and dependable, in a sea of insecurity. You could predict what I was going to do but had the brilliance of imagination to capture your fancy.

I was the anchor in our relationship and you were the sea.

Midori and I rode out tutorials with secret notes and winks and nods. Sometimes we even exchanged names to confuse the hapless fourth year tutors or pretended we were sisters. The buildings were new, the floors had carpet tiles dotted with stock exchange numbers to break out from the grey. We were not that interested in numbers or finance but it impressed our parents, in my case, who knew that money kept them alive.

One boy wonder who had the latest iPad and iPhone still spoke English with a strong mainland Chinese accent. Our prejudice brought us together; we thought he was like a peasant. After stumbling out an invitation to go for coffee, he mercifully clammed up and stayed quiet for most of our classes. Except one.

Midori

That day Midori felt the chill winds blow. She walked into the building, braving the wind tunnel caused by the breezeway on the ground floor. She hoped that her lover would be there first. She did not like the way some of the Asian overseas students looked at her, their eyes like marbles rolling down her chest. Her lover made her strong, strong enough to laugh in their faces. But only when she was there.

The class was assembling as normal. Chen was early but that wasn't unusual. He was seated in the corner rubbing his hands together. The other students looked askance at him and sat a distance away. No one asked him what was wrong. He was the oddball of the class, and every class had one.

"You do not understand me!"

The words are punctuated with gunshots and the metallic smell of blood.

She was frozen to the spot, fixated by the bloody flowers and handprints on the white tiled floor. In the background of her consciousness she heard struggling and the tutor screaming, "Drop it! Drop the gun!"

They were shocked into silence. They gave their statements to the police holding hands. The mobile phone system was overwhelmed on campus, and they missed frantic calls from their families.

Later she would read that their tutor, a 21-year-old Australian honours student, was a hero. He jumped on Chen and held the struggling Chinese student down. Later he would say it was like holding poisonous snakes.

Chen was feeling excluded in the class. Now he faced deportation if he failed. Instead, he would be imprisoned in Australia in a psychiatric facility.

Âu Cô

The building was locked down until the police came. Campus security got to the tutorial room first and relieved the tutor of his captive. Midori sat in the corner of the classroom shaking, her eyes round, staring at the two bodies. I found myself having to be the strong one, holding her as she whimpered.

Shock cocooned me and allowed me to breathe. He had shot the two top students in our class, a Chinese girl and a Singaporean boy. They came first.

When I read about what the police found in his flat, a cold chill ran down my spine. Midori was next for rejecting him when he asked us out for coffee.

Maybe his death wish was what pushed her over. Her world was broken by those gunshots. People were good to her. But the shooting changed that. She became part of my world and her innocence had shattered like the ricocheted glass in the classroom windows.

"We are sorry. We are so sorry," said the Vice Chancellor sharing a poem at the memorial service. So many Australians who had not spoken to her until now share their sorrow.

We are not like this. This is not what Australia is like. She wanted to reassure them.

Australia was freedom from filial piety and societal rules. It was a gentle friendlier place, where people were not so quick to judge. Australia was the tutor who saved Midori from being shot. He was a brunette sports boy who represented the university in long distance running.

It was the Chinese parents and the pressure on their only children that caused Chen to take revenge on his classmates.

Midori would wake screaming and be shocked out of sleep. Midori would have flashbacks, when watching TV, whenever there were sounds of gunshots. Even a clap of thunder would send her cowering.

Too much had happened to her. She tried to spin dragon tales to distract her, but the fantasy fell flat against the stark reality of their world. The dragons were powerless against human evil.

"Âu Cô. Âu Cô," you would call me in the middle of the night. I was your talisman against darkness.

"Don't leave me," you would say and I would stroke your hair gently.

Midori

She pays attention to her little brother who has sprouted legs and peroxide blond hair. The extra attention makes the boy uncomfortable and he starts worrying about his sister.

"Are you all right?"

"Yes."

The polite façade maintained because neither wants to worry the other.

Her brother makes dinner for them both. Somehow he has acquired this skill as well, while they were lost being dragons.

"It was in the paper again today." He gestures over to the coffee table where a newspaper is folded.

"Again?"

She detests the constant reminders. She has stopped going to the university counsellor, she doesn't want to rehash what has happened. Thankfully, it is near the end of semester and they have all been given special consideration and will not need to sit the exam until January.

The first class after the shooting was like a dirge. She wanted to cry, and one of the Australian students did, earning the comfort of the others. Where the two deceased students sat was empty. Someone had brought flowers and they were piled up in front of the classroom to join the other floral tributes outside the building. So many people felt guilt for having survived.

Midori wished he had shot her first.

She had to reach the top of the mountain. She walked through the ascending passage of the red torii gates. Out of breath, she could not ease up and relax even when the fox statues and family tombstones interrupted the torii gates.

Incense floated above her and she found herself bowing to a stone statue of Kannon, the goddess of mercy. She longed for a bowl of noodles and a bottle of Coke to keep her going. But at the Inari mountain shrine the food stallholders were all at the train station. She had to finish her pilgrimage alone.

Somehow she would find her. She waited on the train platform in between the lines for the women-only-carriage. She had to find what she had lost.

Her duet partner clipped her hair back with plastic red bows, kawaii, childlike even though she was over fifteen. Her smile was like a dimple, spontaneous, her eyes crinkling dark and mischievous. She was obedient, and seemed malleable, when she was not. She hid love like it was a dirty secret, and no one would suspect.

Midori adored her and the feelings she brought out in her. She wanted to protect her duet partner. She was the elder in the relationship and felt she could take more than her.

Did she survive the tsunami?

Midori had scanned the message boards and toyed with the idea of posting a message for her.

But she knew that her duet partner's parents would censure and punish her. Midori was now free but her duet partner was not.

The train arrived with the sound of a chime. Midori was jostled but found herself unable to get on the train. The doors slid shut and she was on the wrong side of the doors. Her fingers slid alongside the door windows as the train pulled away.

Âu Cô

The bang of the bullets ricocheted off the walls inside my mind. This time when I heard you scream I acted. I ran in between you and Chen as the gun fired again.

You were cut off mid-shriek and I was left holding you in my arms, your head blown apart like how the Singaporean girl died. I had not been fast enough and you died.

The bang of the bullets triggered me off this time. I ran towards Chen and our tutor collided with me as the three of us fell. The tutor's body jerked and I was unscathed. Chen dropped the gun from surprise and silence fell. My hands were bloody with my incompetence and I saw Chen smile.

The bang of the bullets ripped apart my complacency. I threw myself on Chen and I was shot, searing hot. Your screaming continued in my ears as I floated away.

I knew that I was dreaming. I was lucid dreaming. I had read about it in a book. The dreamer witnessing the dream actually thinks and acts in it. In the grip of it I knew its echoes would be important.

I woke up, my muscles twitching from rushes of adrenalin. Next to me you gently snored. I traced the curve of your cheek with my finger and marvelled we were still alive.

Brother

Sometimes he dreamt of drowning. The water would choke him and rise up his nose. He'd breathe in the water and then would wake up, his heart pounding.

Then he would go to the family shrine in the living room and light incense for his parents who he was sure were trying to tell him something. In the picture, his mother was young and beautiful while his father smiled into the distance as if something pleased him very much.

Maybe they would be happy with him and Midori. They were learning English in Australia and he was proving to be good at pure mathematics. At least with equations the numbers obeyed laws. Unlike people.

He had latched onto his aunt in Tokyo as his guardian since Midori did not have time for him. He told his aunt about Melbourne, the space and the slowness, and about his new friends. She always responded to his email within a day and then he did not feel so alone.

He did not tell her about everything.

The shooting made him grateful to his deceased parents who were surely looking out for his beautiful sister. He tried not to cling to her when she came home with Âu Cô that day, but that night he slept with his soft toy kangaroo for reassurance.

Âu Cô

I stayed overnight with Midori for a week. My aunt said nothing. I explained that Midori was too scared to sleep alone. My aunt suspects nothing, or so we think.

But then my parents come to Melbourne, a marriage proposal in their hands, hoping that I realise that life is too short to delay much longer.

Husband

He was ABV, Australian-Born Vietnamese, and he was comfortable in his skin and the sun. He liked Midori and laughed when he was told her best friend styled herself as Âu Cô.

"Mountain fairy," he joked and was given a wink in return. The two girls bookended each other, finishing each other's sentences and sharing each other's followers. He befriended both of them at the same time over Facebook, and loved the quirky pictures Âu Cô would take with her phone. He was glad that he could be a platonic friend of these girls. The ease of being a fellow undergraduate meant he wasn't automatically targeted as having dating potential.

He did not think that he was as handsome as some of his friends. But he was all right, and he had the confidence of having been in a long-term relationship for over a year before.

Then the shooting happened.

He had frozen before Mark had taken action. Midori's keening cut into the air. The reverberation of the gun shots he had never experienced before.

He had had a beer with the boy who was slaughtered. He had accented English which he apologised for once, and then promptly forgot. The boy was rendered unrecognisable by the gunshot wound to the head.

The girl he had not gotten to know.

What a waste, he thought. He had once helped out Chen with an assignment. That alone probably saved him from being on the list. Chen had struck him as being an eccentric fish out of water. He was a big fish in the town he had come from, but here he was just another lost Asian international student.

It was said of Dzung that he was everybody's friend; well at least he tried.

After the shooting, his father, a refugee from the wars, told him that he now knew what it was like. His mother had cried because he was still alive.

He was the eldest son, head of family and had still not done his duty and produced a family.

He had commiserated with Âu Cô, they both had the same Vietnamese traditions pulling at them. He had numerous drinks with her and Midori. They had the comfort of surviving the shooting together and appreciated the black humour it inspired. Only Âu Cô and Midori seemed to understand his jokes these days.

The pressure increased as the days went by, until finally he wrote to the parents of the girl he got along best with.

Âu Cô

My parents hugged me and felt my arms through teary eyes, glad that I was alive. I tolerated their clinging as proof that they did love me, their only daughter.

Mother changed from being distant to overinvolved, wanting to know if I was eating properly and engaging Midori in deep conversation about what she wanted to do once she graduated. She insisted on being taken to the best South Vietnamese restaurants, and she exclaimed at the bánh xèo, crispy yellow pancake, and the cleanliness of the cafes I took her to.

Father was more prosaic, waiting patiently for mother to eventually bring up the subject of marriage.

Dzung had not told me he had approached my parents. They immediately wanted to know where he was so they could inspect where he lived and what sort of bachelor he was.

I felt cornered. When mother showed me a print out of his email, my heart sank. Dzung was a nice guy. He was Australian but not too Australian, liberal enough to be attracted to me, but knew enough of the old traditions to approach my parents first.

There was no reason for me not to enjoy his courtship.

Except you.

When I told you I was greeted by silence. I plunged on, out of my depth. The undertow of family obligation had me in its grip, and I knew intuitively you would understand, although you may not like it.

How could I say that this would be the only opportunity for me to have a child? That no boy had ever shown me this much attention, unlike the favours that were given to you like lollies to children at a theme park?

"I want a child," I said.

"So do I," you said, and foolishly I thought this was consent.

After the shooting everything was more vivid: the coriander in my pho, the sharp smell of gum trees and cut grass on campus. Each moment of my life seemed more precious, and your life even more so after your close call.

Some days I found myself waking with a smile on my face because I was alive. But I had to hide it from you, for you had withdrawn like when your parents died. There was the same strain to your face and I did not know how to draw you out of yourself. At least that is what I told myself afterwards.

Midori

When her parents died, after the initial shock and loss, a sense of relief crept in on tiny feet. Though outwardly in mourning, she hugged herself and Âu Cô all the tighter. No one was going to make Âu Cô disappear. Her parents could not separate them.

The Vietnamese girl was grounded in a way she was not. Âu Cô was more prosaic and in the here and now, whereas she was building castles in the sky. She allowed herself to love Âu Cô and become attached once her parents had passed on. They were circumspect despite Australia's supposed liberalism; they could not undo the Asian traditions they had grown up with.

And so she thought she understood when Âu Cô told her about the marriage proposal. She thought she could tolerate it as long as Âu Cô didn't love him, and she continued to stay with her.

But the shooting had shattered her complacency. Everything was finite. Love could not last forever if lovers died. And there were evil people out there that were out to get them.

I'm afraid that I might die. Or you might die. What would happen to the dragons then?

Reassurance came that she would live.

In Japanese myths and tales, to take your life was the heroic way out. She had learnt that failing to die made living worse.

You do not know how often I think of taking the last step, she thought at Âu Cô. But she could not say it. She wanted Âu Cô to be happy, and Dzung seemed to make her smile.

What is our relationship? The question would die on her lips, when she saw the engagement ring glittering on Âu Cô's hand.

How could she speak of something so ethereal against something so material and real?

I cannot offer what Dzung can offer you, she thought forlornly as Dzung and Âu Cô shared another short conversation in Vietnamese.

Âu Cô

For some reason I thought that things would not change between us. Even if I was married. I viewed my husband as another part of my family, to be humoured and gotten around.

You had become more withdrawn and miserable. I did not know what to do because I was causing you pain.

"The two people I care about the most are you and my brother."

That sealed the deal for me; my immature heart wanted you to say me and only me. You had talked about your brother as if the little boy was a burden.

Looking back I now understand that he was the closest living relative to your parents. You paid out your guilt in PlayStation games and home cooked meals.

But even this was not enough.

Brother

He was terrified when his newsfeed told him about the shooting. He could not get hold of Midori or her friend for three hours. He felt hollow again until he heard Midori's voice shaking and sobbing.

This time he had run out of tears. He thanked his ancestors and his parents who were surely looking out for Midori. Maybe they had heard his prayers. After all, he didn't want to be the only descendant of their family.

Âu Cô stayed at their apartment for a week. She made up stories about ghosts and dragons to him, and even Midori sat and listened. It was the most he had seen of his sister since he had come to Australia and the happiest he had been since their parents died.

Midori

They spent more time with Âu Cô's fiancé and his best friend Matt. It amused her watching Dzung court Âu Cô and Matt's feigned indifference to her.

Matt was another nice guy who had witnessed the unspeakable with them. When he suggested to go to Lal Lal for the day, the small town he had grown up in, Midori and Âu Cô leapt at the opportunity. He promised that he would show them the bush and kangaroos.

On the car trip, Matt talked about the large waterfall they would see. Lal Lal meant running water in indigenous tongues. And how they would see old mine shafts from the Gold Rush times. He did not mention the purge of Chinese miners and their repatriation in the late nineteenth century. Nor the massacre of indigenous people.

But Âu Cô knew of it regardless. All lands had a bloody history with a force that bashed them all.

They had lunch in Ballarat and then Matt drove them down gravel roads to see the waterfall.

The waterfall was massive, a great gash in the earth. Midori descended to the base of the waterfall closely followed by Matt and the others. She smiled as the cold spray of the water drenched her.

It was her first smile since the shooting. Âu Cô smiled back and a tension she had been holding of worry for Midori released.

"An earth dragon made this waterfall, twisting through the rocks," Midori said.

"The indigenous people say the rainbow serpent made the land the shape it is today," Matt replied. He put his hands in the cold water and splashed it on his face.

"Rainbow dragon," Âu Cô said.

They visited the regional state forest and Matt unerringly led them to a closed mine shaft.

"I used to play here when I was younger. They've only boarded up the shafts in the last couple of years."

Dzung got a stick from the ground and prodded at the wooden planks barring their passage.

Rusted bits of metal lay around the mining site and the red dust covered their shoes.

"They were mining the earth dragon. He left gold in his wake and they mined him," Âu Cô suggested.

Matt opened his mouth and closed it again. It was so close to indigenous mythology that it might even be true.

"You should go to Uluru while you are here. The gullies are huge and at Coober Pedy you can see the remains of opal dragons," Matt said.

"Opal?" Âu Cô asked.

"Pretty gem stones. They are mostly blue with flecks of rainbows in them. You can also get white opals and black ones."

"I'd like to see an opal," suggested Midori. She could see Matt filing away her wish and desire in his mind.

"We'll go to Victoria Market and I'll show you opals," he promised and Midori smiled again, breaking his heart.

On the way back to the car, Matt showed them the round droppings from kangaroos.

He heard a crunch and gestured them to stop and be quiet. Movement twitched from the ferns and two large grey kangaroos stared at the foursome. Then they turned tail and bounced away.

Âu Cô had gotten her phone out too late to take a picture. But the power of their jumping stayed with her for the rest of the day. Midori was all smiles and Âu Cô wished for a moment that she could make her light-hearted again. Their trip to Lal Lal had refreshed them all and it wasn't until they were back having dinner in Melbourne that she realised that an entire day had gone past and there had been no talk of the shooting at all.

Âu Cô

Dzung and I could laugh together, and the conversation flowed like cheap wine. Dzung apologised for approaching my parents first but explained he did not know how he would be received being a Việt Kiều.

I understood his hesitancy.

The North and South divide still existed in people's hearts 35 years later.

He admired my stories that I created for your little brother, of ghosts and magical animals.

I shone in his wonder.

I could not do any better than him, I told you, as I tried on wedding dresses. I wanted a slender gown with a long train and veil like a dragon's tail.

Your face was frozen as if you had sucked on a sour candy.

"I understand. I want you to be happy."

I accepted your endorsement too easily. Of course you wanted me to be happy. I did not understand then the sacrifice you were contemplating for me.

When the Việt Kiều boy proposed marriage to my parents my wings were clipped.

My parents saw the promise of Australian citizenship in his wooing and yielded to his every wish, including giving me away. My whole family's future was at stake, we were not connected to the Party and we could get nowhere in Hanoi.

You did not say anything, and I knew you understood I had to go through with my parents' wishes. This made it worse. You watched as I tried on wedding dresses through my tears. You seemed to be the stronger one, for you did not cry out aloud.

Midori

Someone was stalking her again. Leaving flowers and petals along the sidewalk at uni to remind her of his presence. It was another Asian loser, lost in a fantasy about what a girlfriend would be like, thanks to Japanese anime.

She already knew what a loser, when pushed, was capable of doing.

As she walked home to her apartment, her shoulder twitched.

"I know you. I can give you everything you want."

His voice sounded in her ear and she spun around to confront him but he was already gone. The branches on the gum tree nearby waved as another tram rattled by.

The tram ad read: HAVE YOU FOUND WHAT YOU ARE LOOKING FOR? Another slogan for her university. She was the Asian model they used to represent all international students in their ads.

Midori scurried home and let the door slam on the outside world with relief. Her little brother jumped, he was in the kitchen pouring cereal for an afternoon snack.

She ignored him, he was a spy for their parents. She went into her room, closed the door. Putting down her bag she slumped down on the bed, curling up in her quilt. Then she tucked in her chin, waiting for Âu Cô to call.

Âu Cô

"I was afraid that my parents had taken you away."

"I'm still here. I'll come over."

I put the phone down. I didn't want to remind you over the phone that your parents are dead. Feeling slightly guilty for coming home first before calling you, I walked through the large park that separated you and me. The evening sky was a dusky pink. Melbourne had only a tinge of smog that made the sunsets beautiful.

I breathed in the gum leaves of the park and was glad I did not do what my parents suggested and return to Vietnam straight away. There were still good things about Australia and you were one of them.

When I knocked on your door I was received by your little brother. For the first time I realised how large his eyes were in a skinny face, there was no chubbiness about him at all.

"She's in there," he says with a slight cough.

"Arigato. Thank you." I bow my head and take off my shoes to put in the rack beside the door.

Knocking on your bedroom door I suddenly wondered what I would do if you did not open it.

The thought was swept out of my mind as you opened the door. You were dishevelled, you had been sleeping in your clothes but you still had a jaunt to your hip, even a shooting couldn't keep you down for long.

"Some other bastard has been following me," you say straight to the point before I could even sit down.

"Who?"

"Chen, no not Chen. Chan. Or Chong. Chinese anyway."

I skip over the surname problem.

"Is he from uni?"

"Yes. One of the Asians. He wants a girlfriend. I don't want to be anyone's girlfriend! Not any boy's girlfriend anyway."

I take your slim white hands in mine. They are shaking.

"I've been feeling sick. The world goes wheeeee ..."

I grab your hands as you try to gesticulate.

"Calm down. Have you had something to eat or drink?"

"No. My brother, the little pest tells my parents about everything I do. I don't trust him. He may be trying to poison me so he gets all our inheritance."

"Your parents ..." I trailed off. The inkling I had that something was amiss had become a huge question in my mind.

Your eyes were closing as if you were very tired. I sat by you as you drifted off to sleep.

When I was certain that you were asleep I loosened your grip on my fingers and slipped out.

You sounded like you had taken drugs or pills.

I opened up your university bag to see if any clues were there.

Mobile, wallet, e-reader. Diary. Receipts, a phone bill.

It was as if you were drugged. Feeling as if I was betraying a confidence, I walked out into the lounge room where I thought I heard your little brother.

He was there with headphones clamped around his ears as he typed on his MacBook.

"Hello? Midori is asleep. Have you noticed anything odd about her?"

Your little brother looked at me as if he was just waking from an electronic dream.

"No. She doesn't talk. I mean she doesn't talk to me."

"OK."

I retreated back to your bedroom. I typed 'overdose' in a search engine with my laptop and came upon a drug crisis line for Australia.

Ringing the advice line I rehearsed in my mind what I was going to say.

My friend Midori's parents died in the tsunami and today she thinks they are still alive.

No I don't know if she has taken anything. I've rummaged through her bag. She is asleep now.

I felt like a traitor, talking about you behind your back.

But I was out of my depth and the counselling service at the university was closed.

They gave me another number to ring.

It was only afterwards that I realised it was a psychiatric hospital's phone number.

Midori

She woke up groggy as if from a long sleep.

Âu Cô was sitting next to her, reading a document on her laptop.

She blinked and night seemed to have invaded her room. The rescue helicopter had pulled her from the floods and only she had survived. The tsunami swept from under her and it was as if her hands were conducting the spread of the waves.

"How are you?" Âu Cô asked and before she could answer, water had filled her mouth and she was sinking, sinking away.

Another blink and Midori can see the ceiling and the face of the university counsellor above her. They carry her from the room. Chen was sitting in tutorial class alone as usual. The rest of the class were talking oblivious until she took out a handgun and shot him. His blood and the wound were gory and revolting to behold.

Her hands were sticky with blood and the gun was hot to the touch.

She was eating dinner with her little brother and Âu Cô. The flat was bugged by the police and she knew she could not let on that they were being bugged. Chen shot the two agents in the classroom and she was the third. Her parents died in the line of fire and she nearly had as well.

She could only trust Âu Cô with her interests. Even her brother was a spy, a monitor of her.

The doorbell rang and she covered her mouth with her hand. Secrets were peeling away from her unspoken.

Âu Cô answered the door and the two middle aged people standing there worked for the government. Midori recognised them from hanging around at the university.

"We need to ask you a few questions," they said.

Midori could predict what they were going to say. Name, address, phone number, university affiliation.

She even could predict Âu Cô's questions of them.

What could they do to help?

What happens now?

I know them, Midori wanted to say. *It's nothing to worry about they are my friends.*

Âu Cô

I stood by helpless as they questioned you. As you started to talk about how your brother was a spy for your parents, I looked to him wondering if I should have gotten him out of the kitchen first.

Then when you said you had murdered Chen with a handgun, I saw wariness come into their eyes. One of them stepped out of the apartment to make phone calls.

"Does she have a weapon?" one of them asked me.

I shook my head hoping I was right. I didn't know if I could trust these people. The woman seemed nice enough, she reminded me of a nurse with her manner.

"Don't worry, Âu Cô. These are my friends," you told me and tears came to my eyes. There was something wrong with you and I could not fix it.

Mutely I nodded. The woman took the effort to explain to Midori and me what was happening.

"Midori, do you feel well?" she asked you.

You said you were fine. Except you were hyperactive.

She then turned to me.

"How do you think Midori is going?"

Feeling like a traitor I opened my mouth and closed it again.

"It's better if you are honest," the woman said.

"Nothing Midori says makes any sense. That's why I called the help line. It's as if she is drugged or something."

The woman nodded, as if confirming her suspicions.

She told Midori, "We are ringing to see if there is a hospital ward where you can be looked after. You can stay there over the weekend. Your friend can visit you in the afternoon and evening."

She scribbled down an address on a piece of paper.

"Can you pack a bag for her? I'm going to talk with Midori a little more."

I reluctantly retreated to your room, wiping my eyes with the back of my hand.

Midori

The very nice people took her for a ride in an ambulance. Through the windows she could see the bright red lights flashing against the traffic and the trees.

In the hospital ward they gave her some tablets and watched her swallow them. Then she went to sleep.

When Midori woke up the first thing she felt was relief. She had not killed anybody and she was not in jail. She got up and opened the door of her single room into the brown dimly-lit corridor in her pyjamas. A nurse stepped into the corridor.

"Breakfast, Midori," the nurse said.

When she tried to walk outside the ward she was stopped. Then she realised she wasn't in jail but somewhere else. Through the nurses' station she could see into another part of the ward where nurses were in uniform and the people were wan and listless.

She tried to smile at the nurse in the lounge but her facial muscles wouldn't move. She blinked at him instead.

What was the point of surviving to be like this? she wondered. She wandered back into her room to look in her bag. Âu Cô had packed her a soft toy sun with large black eyes. It was the toy Âu Cô had given her after the shooting. *Cheer up*, the toy would say.

Âu Cô

When I got back home I burst into tears again. You were sick, sick in the head from what I could work out. I only knew the words in English. No one at home in Vietnam would get sick like this, or so I thought.

If I thought too much about what you were saying my mind would be repelled by you. None of it made any sense.

Your little brother had assured me he was going to be all right so I left him on his own in your apartment. I didn't know what to say to my aunt, so I said you were ill and had to be taken to hospital. "They didn't know what was wrong," I said, though I suspected they knew something that they weren't telling me.

I needed to talk to someone about what happened. An Australian who could make sense of it all.

That was when I called Dzung for the first time of my own accord, to help me put things together.

Husband

Dzung was saddened by what had happened to Midori, but was glad he could help Âu Cô. They became closer as Midori stayed on in hospital for a week. For the first time, he saw Âu Cô cry, and Midori speechless.

He had a grandfather with post-traumatic stress disorder, or schizophrenia, depending on who the doctor was. He thought that the shooting had driven Midori crazy.

It made him double-check his own reality, which was rock solid, and Âu Cô, who seemed sane. They attended the memorial service for the two deceased students together, and he put his arm around her when she leaned her head on his shoulder. The tutorial group seemed to accept their closeness, and Midori's illness, with equanimity or shock, it was hard to tell which.

Midori

She exited from hospital sober and solemn. Smiles did not come as readily to her any more and she had lost her bounce. She should have been alert to the fact that Âu Cô would come with Dzung to escort her home, but she was grateful that anyone had come at all, given how sick she had been.

Dzung and her little brother had prepared lunch and she tried to smile but could not. Dzung had then left to go to uni and Âu Cô remained with her, as if things were the same as ever.

"Thank you for standing by me," she whispered in Âu Cô's arms, and Âu Cô smiled the smile that she could not, happiness and contentment all together.

Âu Cô

Dzung would take us places and it seemed he did not know how close we really were. We would go in a foursome, me and you, Dzung and his best friend Matt. The shooting was what brought us together, so it seemed. Matt would make jokes that were funny at first, and then grow sad as we sobered up after the giddiness of still being alive.

Dzung and Matt wanted to show us the bush again and we went to Hanging Rock once. You could not see the attraction until Matt told us the story about the four girls who had disappeared. Then by the time we reached the rock we were both spooked and scared.

The Rock was not large compared to the mountains at home, but I felt from it the same pull and power. The eucalypts were especially sharp here, among the damp moss.

It started raining slightly and mist seemed to rise from the earth as the clouds closed in.

My hand closed over yours, and I squeezed you gently.

"Earth dragon," you whispered in my ear as we followed the boys back to the car.

"Mountain fairy," I replied. If there were mountain fairies in Australia surely they would hide in a place like this.

It was a story-book courtship. My parents had been won over first, by his tidy apartment and his promise of a graduate job.

Then I found myself going to movies, going rock climbing, going camping. Sometimes you even came along and he did not mind that you and I were closer than him and I.

Our close brush with death made me even more prone to please my parents and give them the grandchild they wanted. And Dzung was the rock I was looking for when you were ill.

I stayed over at your apartment less frequently now. I took for granted that you were always available to see me until one day you were not.

> Once there was a wind dragon who fell in love with a musician who played the guitar at the edge of a pier that looked out to sea. She would drop down on the sound of his strummed chords and whistle in time to the music of her body.
>
> The gods said she could retain human form if she gave up her immortality to be with him.

This story made you angry. "Why did the dragon have to give up her true nature to be with a man?"

"She didn't have to," I explained, caught mid-sentence. "We can make it that he has to sacrifice himself to be with her."

"As if that would actually happen," you said. Real life was intruding on our story making. I had never seen you so angry.

"Men might do it if they were in love," I speculated but this did not sooth you.

"I would not do it for a man," you said, your lips in a line and I knew better, or so I thought then, to inquire any further.

If I had known then your silence was not consent.

If I had followed my desires and said I wanted you rather than him, if I had put my family aside, would you have still loved me?

These questions have no answers. They are just my wonderings in the wind.

Midori

She was out of hospital for a month before the wedding. She wished to be steampunk and wear black lace. But the bridesmaid gown was already chosen and tailored to her measurements.

The fiancé, naïve and only thinking the best of her lover, let them meet up late at night and stay at each other's houses. She is unable to hate him; he is so gormless with that childish honour and simplicity that reminds her of her brother before her parents died. He is like a child, nothing bad had happened for him to see the world in shades of grey. Everything at face value. And she is just her lover's best friend.

He and her lover speak Vietnamese to each other and it makes her aware that there is a whole world in Vietnam that she has not seen. Merely glimpsed in the taste of pho restaurants and Facebook photos.

Maybe her lover's family would die too – in a typhoon – she decides one lonely night. Then she would be free like Midori. Maybe.

Husband

He finally yielded to his parents' incessant nagging and took Âu Cô home to meet them. He could tell that his mother had to swallow her prejudice when Âu Cô spoke with a northern accent.

As the days went by he found more to like and even love about Âu Cô. She wanted children like he did and she had flights of fancy that manifested in little kindnesses, like the stories she told Midori's little brother. The deep friendship she had with Midori warmed him to both of them, friendship was something he valued from Australians and Vietnamese alike. When he asked his friend Matt to be his best man, the boy cried.

In return he had planned a huge buck's night, where the best man did the most drinking and throwing up afterwards.

Âu Cô

The week before the wedding I came to your apartment as usual. Ringing the doorbell no one answered for a long time. My heart felt a premonition of something bad about to occur. Last time your brother found your body. What would happen if I did?

The door opened on your little brother. He looked up at me sorrowfully.

"Midori has gone away," he said.

"Gone away! Why? How come?" All these questions rushed to my lips.

"She left you a letter. Come in," your brother said.

"Has she left you on your own?"

The little boy nodded.

"She's gone to New South Wales. To mountains. Not very far."

I followed him into the living area and I saw the letter propped up on the dining table. Like you, it was clean cut with cherry blossoms embossed on it. I opened the letter, my heart sinking.

> *I am writing to you so you know what is real from the bottom of my heart. I cannot watch and wait for you as you get married to have your child. I have gone to the Blue Mountains to ease the pain.*
>
> *Please don't try to follow me or contact me. I have turned off my mobile and will not access email. I still feel the same way about you as I did when we first met. That is how come I cannot be your bridesmaid and smile for your family. As I write this I'm beginning to cry. I want you to be happy and I hope that you are. Love Midori.*

Your writing in English was neat and precise. Your depth of feeling for me and what you were prepared to sacrifice for my happiness took my breath away.

I was buoyant on that feeling for a moment, and then your absence took hold of my heart.

I missed you, and I realised I needed you to get through the marriage ceremony.

Had I made a mistake?

How could I throw away everything for love? A love so much like the fairy tales we fed on that it was unreal. Like the heroine of a folk tale I had a choice, to give up everything for the unknown, the romantic, a choice of the heart.

But I did not live in a fairy-tale world. My doting parents were buying a house in Australia for us to live in. My fiancé had given me a diamond band engagement ring. Midori was a student who could offer me nothing after the tsunami. My parents would disown me for the shame of it. Midori could not offer me a home in Japan or Australia. And she had just been seriously ill in the mind.

All we had were the stories that bound us together. But I could not live in a fantasy, and I hardened my heart.

Midori wrote me a long email that appeared in my inbox in the early morning.

We still see the same stars and the same rabbit in the moon. Out here the stars shine more brilliantly in the pitch darkness of the night. I imagine you watching Earth's satellites holding my hand.

Yesterday I felt the call of the wind down the valley of the mountains. The cliffs are orange here from the iron content of the soil. White birds soar on the winds, up and down calling to each other.

The words tug at my heart. I can see myself there, but again my thoughts return to my family. I could run away to Katoomba, the town that postmarks Midori's letters, but I would let everybody down.

Âu Cô

The day before my wedding was when I finally broke down in front of him.

"Do you still want to marry me?" he asked with brown cow eyes.

"Yes," I said. What else could I say? The wedding was booked, the reception was planned and my parents had flown to Australia to see me get married.

I did not tell him that I had cried in your arms the week before. You were the one bridesmaid, dressed in gold. I had not had the time to make many other friends. You were everything to me.

You could not bear it, you admitted finally. The words that might have made me protest other people's plans for me.

"I want a child," I told you. "My parents want to move here with my sister. This is the only way." *I want to make everyone happy*, was what I did not say because it wasn't true. I was not happy and neither were you.

My mother ends up being the matron of honour and her happiness is too much for me to bear. She delights in the company of Dzung's parents and family and tugs on the zip of my wedding dress too tightly.

"I'm so proud of you," she whispers smiling with red lipstick lips.

I let her and father and sister sweep me up in their celebration in preparation for when the groom comes to fetch the bride.

When Dzung arrives with his groomsmen, his brother and Matt he winks at me. I suppress the smile that rises to my lips. Only my mother and sister hover. I have made no other close friends in Australia. I invited my economics class to the reception and the tutor to ensure the tables are balanced, no more.

When Dzung asks me where you are, I lie and say you were jealous of my good fortune and could not bear to be at my wedding. Maybe in some way it is true.

The necklace of silver and rubies weighs heavily around my neck as we listen to the civil ceremony. When it comes to the vows, I repeat the serious words that he has composed. I had let him plan the wedding, I merely agreed to the date.

When I say that I will love and cherish him, involuntarily I think of you.

The moment when you could have protested comes and goes. A hope in me dies that you may have changed your mind and come back to Melbourne.

Love is supposed to change everything and transform you. You have made me beautiful, so Dzung would be interested in me. He said he loves me because of my liveliness and imagination. He does not know how much of it is due to you. And now without you, my face has become stark like white chalk make-up. Tears threaten where joy used to spring.

And on this day of days which is supposed to define my life forever, I want to run and hide.

When I say I do, I feel smothered. Smothered by his good intentions. Everything exciting that has happened in my life has occurred and looking forward I see a world blanketed only by his will.

I cry and lie that it is for joy.

During the reception I can only imagine your commentary and how dragons would sweep the red decorations away with the flick of a tail. My mother and father beam at the richness of the meal that follows, the Peking Duck, the stuffed yams, the roast abalone, seafood hotpot and many others.

I drink champagne and barely manage the toasts at each table. It is perfect, like everything else about Dzung.

At the table with our economics class we are effusively embraced. They accept that Midori is sick and could not come. It seems more special to me, sharing these better moments with the people who had shared the worst moments of my life. Even though we had not seen each other for a few weeks, they are close like brethren.

And they are drunk, drunk on the absences of those who are not here. Somehow only what they feel is real to me, and their emotions are what I can now relate to. Like war veterans we stand in silence, saluting those who were lost.

Dzung kisses me, anchoring me to the ground, and I am grateful.

We exit to the sound of music by Brahms and we go to the hotel that overlooks the city. It glistens like dragon's pearls in the night.

He is gentle with me, and I pant a little when he does what you do to me so well. But when he enters me and comes I feel nothing and pat him on the head.

He falls asleep easily and I'm left looking outside at the city lights wondering if the dragons rise and fall in the rain.

It's my memories that make me able to tolerate his touch. Perhaps there was something wrong with me that after you left I had no interest in boys or even girls. Perhaps there was only one person in the world who could make me feel that special. You were the only one. I could not imagine being touched by anyone else.

Dzung was nice enough, his eyes slightly wide set. He was polite and had a sense of humour although it was put on sometimes. I do not know why he gently persisted. Was he delusional like the boys who used to chase us with their extravagant declarations of love based only on a glimpse in a window, or the shortest of conversations?

What did he see in me?

How could he live up to you, my lover who knew every part of me after hours of chats and knew exactly what questions to ask when I left silence hanging?

The honeymoon we spend on islands off the Queensland coast. The weather is gently warm, and so is the ocean. I see an eagle ray, a sting ray that leaps over the side of the yacht we hire for the day.

I wear a new bathing suit and feel like someone new, different. When we come home it will be to a new house out in the suburbs. I have inspected it, it is beautiful and large with a garden. It will make it easier to forget about you.

On the third day there is a message on my mobile. It is your little brother wanting to talk to me about you.

With trepidation I ring the number. When he answers I know something is wrong.

"How is Midori?"

The little boy bursts into tears.

"She's gone missing. They found her shoes on a bush track on the cliffs and they think..."

There is roaring in my head like the pounding of the ocean.

Midori

The sharp eucalyptus air braces her lungs as she wanders down the track at the base of the cliffs. Bellbirds call and her sneakers squelch in the muddy puddles after rain.

She feels sheared off from her Japanese self. Alone in the mountains she is finally back to her true nature and she whistles with her joy. No expectations are holding her up any more, and she is free even from the need in her lover's eyes.

Around her the sheer orange cliffs ascend to the blue sky. The Three Sisters tower above her, three rock formations of frozen women. This is the Australia she has dreamed about, not the urban tram-tracked life in Melbourne. The winds blow against her cheeks and she dares to lean over at the lookouts and feel the drop of the waterfalls below.

At night time the most popular route is lit, and it is easy to wander off the beaten track with the stars glittering overhead, the rabbit in the moon looking down upon her.

She has written all this down in email prose, her last adventure.

Reaching the lookout, fenced by metal poles, she clambers over the barrier to precariously walk along the rim of the cliff. Far in the distance she can hear the cooee of other tourists.

She takes off her sneakers and places them next to a bush.

Then she swan dives off the cliff, her face turned to the breeze.

Her body falls and suddenly she feels herself flying upwards, her tail swishing in the wind.

Âu Cô

I followed your trail up to the Blue Mountains. Walking on the same paths, under the same moon. When I looked down the orange-brown cliffs I felt vertigo and then I almost understand.

The gum trees sway gently in the breeze while eucalyptus mist shimmers in the hot air. For a moment a wind dragon brushes my cheek and whispers.

I stop at the lookout where the police had found your sneakers, perfectly paired at the edge of the cliffs. Many Japanese suicide here, and we only know so because they leave their shoes behind, I was told.

Why did you leave me?

I cannot blame you for not wanting to be there when I got married.

What a waste. We had survived together and then you completed Chen's work for him.

I walked around the edge of the cliffs, staying on the path. A white cockatoo called out to its mate and dipped into the gorge on the downwinds. It took my breath away as it floated upon the draft.

This was what you were missing. What you would never see again.

I clenched my fist in my parka. Life was affirmed to me in this beautiful landscape.

I did not want to join you.

I claimed back your effects from the police. There was finality going through your backpack. I wished then I had not come up alone. You only had packed for only two nights. Your writing book was there, heavy and fraught with secrets. All in kanji.

Your brother was your next of kin and I had no rights. Only a signed piece of paper by your brother entitled me to bring the backpack to Melbourne. I was invisible and for a moment I had a taste of what it must have been like for you with the lead up to my wedding.

Brother

He is awash at sea, as if his spirit has been swamped by the tsunami.

His beautiful sister is gone, leaving him to carry on the family ashes. He does not want to live on his own in Australia or Japan. The shock of it makes him cling again to his kangaroo soft toy, the only constant left in his life.

Mother, father and sister.

Why had she gone? She had escaped death once already only to invite it back to her doorstep. He cannot imagine how sad she must have been to not remember that he needed her too.

His favourite aunt is coming to fetch him back to Tokyo. She says that Fukushima has not recovered, that it would be better to stay with her in the city.

He cannot find it in himself to disagree. He loves his aunt and wishes with all his heart that she does not die. He wishes on the moon and the stars now. His ancestors had let Midori go and failed to protect his parents.

At least in Tokyo there are anime fairs and specialty shops, he tells himself, in the dark hollow of the night when he is all alone, squeezing his kangaroo for company. He cannot depend on people, they disappear when you need them. But the moon and stars are always there.

Âu Cô

I went to the beach. Barefoot, the slippery rocks and rough sand on my skin reminded me I was still alive. The winter wind was cold and sharply salted and the ocean was grey like my mood. Sometimes the sun would break through the clouds and the sea would reflect blue again. But this failed to give me hope.

The wind dragons descended on the drafts, brush my cheeks then ascend with a gust of air. They reminded me of my lost freedom, and the flights I could no longer take. Stranded on the ground I leaned into the wind, reddening my cheeks.

I was stunned by your death. You left your little brother behind. You left me behind.

When you said forever, I believed you. Forever did not mean a premature end.

How can I answer your brother's questions? I did not know what was going through your mind, how hurt you must have been from all of it, my wedding, the shooting.

I blamed Chen. He had wanted you dead. You had died. When I looked at my guilt at being married I recoiled at the darkness I had buried inside. Quickly I looked away so I could stay sane.

We caught the first plane back to Melbourne. Dzung drove me to your apartment and stood by the front door like a sentinel while I gave your brother a cuddle. My gaze was drawn to the family shrine and there was an empty photo frame standing between the portraits of your parents. Fresh flowers adorned the shrine and the smell of stale incense dominated the apartment.

When I looked at your brother now I recognised the same plane in his face, of sharp cheekbones.

I was blind to it before, but now I was reaching for anything that could remind me of you.

We cried together and Dzung hugged me, and then your little brother.

“I haven’t been in her room,” the little boy snuffled.

“When is your aunt coming?” I asked him.

“Tomorrow.”

“I’ll look in her room. She may have left something.” Suddenly I wished that Dzung wasn’t there. I realised I wanted to take everything about our relationship so her aunt would not know of it.

You are free, I said to you in my mind. *Finally free.*

Dzung sat down at the kitchen table and patted the chair next to him for your little brother to sit on. They played cards as I opened up your room.

It smelt of your deodorant and tears came to my eyes. The bed was made and squeaky clean with peach-coloured sheets. The desk seemed impossibly tidy. There were pictures of us stuck to the wall including one that I treasured. Dzung had taken it when we were down at the beach, the two of us grinning broadly in front of a sloppy sandcastle.

I sat on the bed. This was where we had made love so many times, each time worth mentioning.

I found myself twisting my wedding ring with my fingers. When Dzung touched me I felt fake. But now there was no one else.

Swallowing back my tears I opened one of the desk drawers. It was a mess. I recognised cards I had given you, stacks of notes, and stationery. Reluctantly I plucked out the cards I could recognise. At the bottom of the drawer was another pile of cards with a rubber band around it. Dust came away at my fingertips.

Despite my misgivings I took out the first card, with a moon and a rabbit on it. If this was who I thought it was from, I had to hide all of them from your family.

It was in kanji and I recognised 愛 ai and the love hearts circling around your name.

I was surprised at myself.

Instead of the jealousy I thought I would feel, I felt a glow of happiness that she had loved you too.

Carefully, I put aside your keepsakes into a paper shopping bag, as if they were you.

Shuffling through the familiar cards that I had written, I found a small notebook. The contents were in Japanese. My first impulse was to ask your brother to translate it for me. Then I puzzled over whether the contents would be ones that I would want shared with him and his family.

Finally the fact that once I left the apartment it would be hard to find a cheap Japanese interpreter made up my mind.

"Little brother," I called, poking my head out of the door of the room.

"There is a Japanese notebook here. I don't know if it is a diary or stories."

The boy's face lit up at the mention of stories. Dzung leaned back in his chair and stretched as I came out holding the key to your heart.

Your brother flipped the notebook open.

"They are stories. I can read them to you in English but slowly."

"Please do," I told him.

There was a dragon who had caused a wave. She was just playing in her mind and heart but her body rippled in the ocean. A tsunami ripped through the sand and crashed onto the shore, killing and wiping out an entire village. As punishment the little dragon began to eat river stones. They sank to the bottom of her belly and she dragged herself to shore every now and again to see what damage the tsunami had wrought. A wind dragon saw how much the little dragon suffered, weighed down by guilt. So the wind dragon came down to kiss the sandy shore and the little water dragon to help her with her burden. The water dragon lapped up the kindness of the wind dragon and felt better.

The wind dragon absolved the water dragon of her guilt, saying that intention was all. The water dragon did not mean to hurt people so she did not have to pay penance for it. Upon hearing this, the water dragon lightened and began to ride the top of the waves to the shore. Upon seeing how the village began to regrow, she was so light that she took off from the crest of the waves and flew away.

The positive message behind your story gave me heart until the reality of your final act crashed in upon me again. Part of me did not want to hear any more of your stories, but my curiosity got the better of me.

There once was a water dragon who spied a prince that walked on land. The prince was handsome and had everything a human woman could want. The water dragon took human form, knowing she could entice him with the gift of her pearl. She waited on the beach of the seashore, murmuring beautiful poetry to herself. The prince saw her and fell in love. But he was not the only creature in love with the now human dragon. Another water dragon who had the same nature loved the human dragon too. She shadowed her and they played games with poetry but she could not offer the water dragon a palace or children. She sacrificed her voice to a witch so she could walk on land with the water dragon and the prince. On the day of their wedding the water dragon tried to sing, and demonstrate her love but no noise came from her throat. The now-human dragon, misunderstanding what the water dragon wanted, gave her a book of their poetry. That night in despair the water dragon threw the book of poetry into the water, and threw herself off a cliff.

In the morning and forever after if you listened to the wind you would hear the water dragon's poetry.

My eyes wet with tears, I reached for Dzung's comforting arms. He seemed puzzled. Your little brother took it in his stride, and blew his nose.

"Was she in love with you?" Dzung asked, half to himself.

"I don't know," I said helplessly.

He pinned me with his gaze, shrewd and compassionate.

"You can tell me the truth. She has gone to the other shore," he said.

I opened my mouth then closed it again. I yearned to tell him, but the consequences ...

"She was my best friend," I said. "No more and no less than that."

"I told Matt I loved him at my buck's night. When I was very very drunk." Dzung laughed and this dissolved the tension that had been building up.

"I understand that friends can love each other," he continued. "It's okay."

At his words I cried for the first time without reservation. It was at that point that my regard for him transformed from fondness into love.

I observe the 49 days of mourning in the Vietnamese Buddhist tradition. Dzung understands when I stay to look after your little brother until your aunt arrives from Japan. The aunt thanks me in stilted English and your little brother tells me that they will have a memorial service in Japan because they cannot find your body in Katoomba.

Your little brother seems dazed and lost, and he takes my hand like he is just a toddler.

I worry about him, he is the last one left of his family. But the aunt who is putting a smile on his face with little quips in Japanese seems capable enough.

When they leave for the airport, he gives me a brief hug, which I treasure as he clambers into the taxi with his aunt.

Dzung does not mind when your picture is placed on our home shrine. He forgives me my tears, and my reluctance to be intimate with him. I know I have to eventually share my body with him again, but it feels impassable now.

Like a kinetic ghost I can feel your embrace around me when I'm alone. In the middle of my days I would be reminded of wind dragons by the breeze. Or the taste of sushi would bring back images of you laughing at my jokes, smiling and winking.

You are depressed, a doctor says after I fill in a quiz.

Inside I'm still in mourning for you. I remember the aunt who came to take your brother away, who took me out for dinner as a thank you for looking after your effects. The police have still not found your body, and I guess privately that they would not have tried very hard amongst the crumbling cliffs and bushland.

The survivors of the shooting hold another memorial service, this time for you. We stand around the rectangular reflection pond, looking into the grey concrete water. I lay a wreath, and pluck a yellow rose from it to float on the surface of the water.

"She was sick before she died, wasn't she?" Matt asks me. I don't consider how he knows. "Such a waste." He shakes his head and pulls out a cigarette.

Dzung holds me and I yield to him. There is nothing stopping me from giving him all of my affection now that you are gone.

"I wish I had made the effort to stay in contact with her," one of the other Singaporean girls said. "Maybe we could have done something."

She names the guilt nagging at me, and I feel myself sinking like a water dragon eating stones.

"What happened isn't your fault," Dzung says and a clenched fist inside me relaxes. "She was unwell."

"I'll remind myself of that," I told him before dissolving again into lonely tears. He did not know what I meant to her. She left no note but her feelings were unequivocal. She loved me and needed me and I was no longer there.

When my belly swells in pregnancy, my husband is delighted.

I feel flat as I waddle around Footscray where the southern Vietnamese go for pho. The baby is a necessity and reminds me too much of what is lost.

My body takes on a rotund shape of its own, and when the ultrasound reveals that the baby is a boy, my family and Dzung's are delighted. Dzung is solicitous of me and tolerates my nausea and grumpiness. When the doctor says I have prenatal depression neither of us is surprised.

"How much is too sad?" the counsellor asks, as I begin to cry for you yet again.

You were my true love, I admit finally to myself.

"What do you feel for Dzung?"

"He is kind to me and a good man."

"Can you feel love for him and Midori?"

The question floors me. I did not know it was possible to love both. I always felt I had to choose.

Husband

He had thought their lives had proceeded as usual as if they were still students except they were living together. He finds it hard to think of Âu Cô as a wife until she is pregnant with their son. Then the reality of what marriage is crashes down on him.

When Midori died he watched Âu Cô collapse in upon herself. She withdrew and all he could do was hold her and wait for her to come back to him. The death of Midori on top of the deaths of the two others in his class made his days seem bleaker. Without Âu Cô's merry laugh and wild stories he found he had less to smile about.

He continues working and it is only the hope of having a son and their own family that keeps him going. Maybe once their son is born, Âu Cô would come back to the world and him again.

Âu Cô

I continue to write stories and send them in emails to your little brother. Over the distance I cannot tell if his replies are genuine or just him being polite. But his gesture makes me feel better, as if by accessing the muse I am touching you again.

It is one of those rare hot summer days that I summon up the energy to go to the beach. The crunching of sand under my feet and the scent of suntan lotion mixed with salt reminds me of you. When I plunge into the cold sea water, a shiver runs up my spine. When I swim, I'm buoyant as if the weight of my pregnant belly is no longer there.

I feel like myself for the first time in a long time. Breathing in, I feel the chill of the sea air. Breathing out I feel the caress of a water dragon around my legs. Floating, the water dragon carries me gently to shore.

A Caesarean section occurs in a blink of an eye as the morphine swamps my unconscious.

When I wake, the baby is sitting on my shoulder with round solemn brown eyes. I cannot help myself and struggle to hold the little wizened creature, supported by Dzung and his mother.

When the baby comes home I wade through sleepless nights and tired blurry days. Living from hour to hour, feeling overwhelmed and swamped by the needs of the baby. Dzung has to go back to work, and I'm rendered incapable of thinking much about you or myself any more.

Some days I look at his large dark eyes lined with long eyelashes and I feel a wrench of love. Nothing like the highs I feel for you or the fondness I have for Dzung, this love is enveloping and grounded in the little baby's needs. All other emotions are swept out of the way with my feelings for my first child. Nothing else seems to matter.

Then one day I'm sitting on the playmat with the baby, watching him pummel the air with his fists and feet. The baby scratches behind his neck and I peer around on the pink skin, wondering what is itchy.

Then I see it, confirming my true nature.

The little baby has silver scales cascading down the back of his neck.

First published by Spinifex Press 2015

Spinifex Press Pty Ltd
504 Queensberry St
North Melbourne, Victoria 3051
Australia
women@spinifexpress.com.au
www.spinifexpress.com.au

Cover design by Deb Snibson, MAPG
Typeset by Deb Snibson
Printed by McPherson's Printing Group

National Library of Australia Cataloguing-in-Publication entry
Pham, Hoa, 1972- author.
Wave / Hoa Pham.
9781742199689 (paperback)
9781742199658 (ebook : epub)
9781742199634 (ebook : pdf)
9781742199641 (ebook : Kindle)
Psychic trauma--Fiction.
Interpersonal relations--Fiction.
Ecofiction.
A823.3

MIX
Paper from responsible sources
FSC® C001695
www.fsc.org